One Tiny Turtle

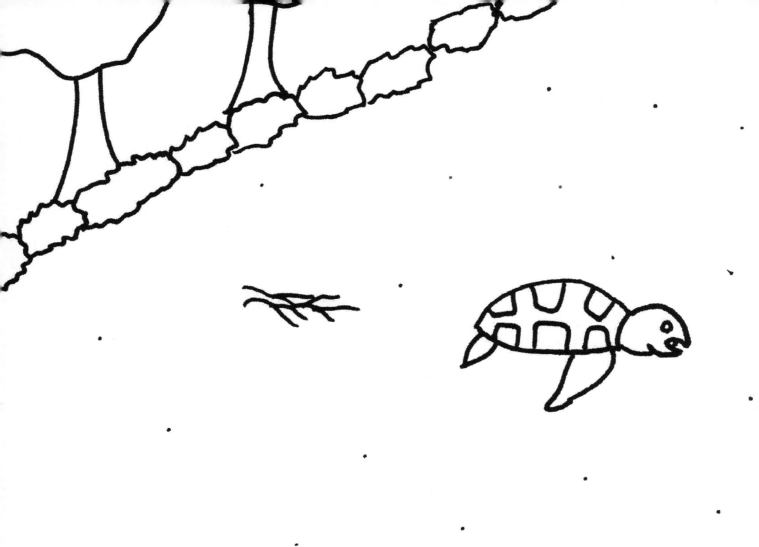

One Tiny Turtle

A Story You Can Colour

Christina Van Starkenburg

ISBN-13: 978-1717470423

ISBN-10: 1717470424

For Allison and Jo-Anne. Without the two of you, this book would not exist.

Up on the beach a small egg hatches.

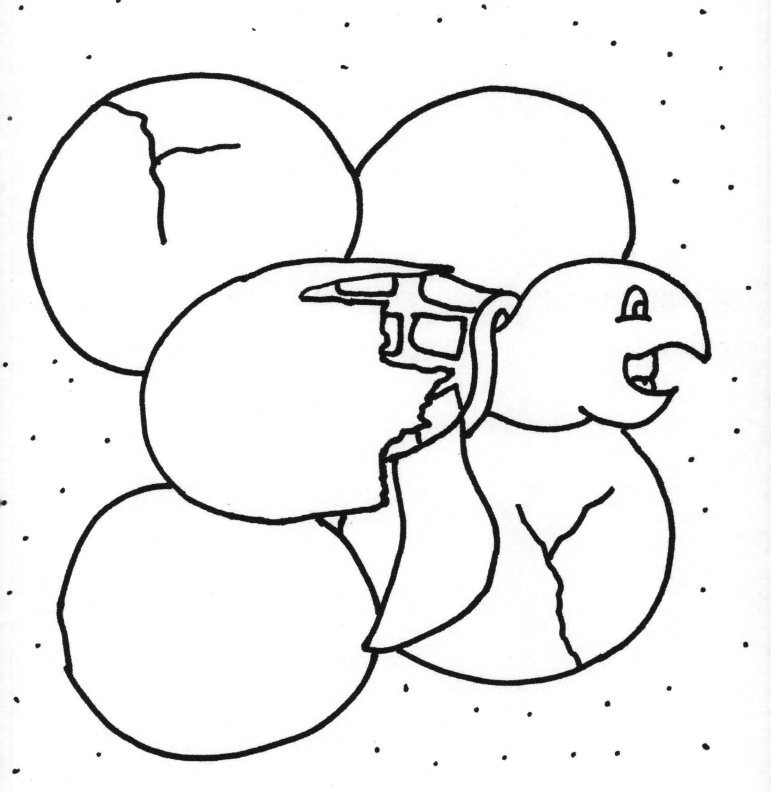

A tiny turtle crawls down to where the wave splashes.

One tiny turtle swims out to sea.

She's excited to learn where her family might be.

She passes two clams shut up in their shells. Anchored tightly to rocks to stay safe in the swells.

Three starfish slowly walk by.

Too busy to notice her, or even say hi.

Then, floating past like a shimmering wish,
She notices four jellyfish.

5

Lost in the reeds she follows the trails

Of five happy and hungry, tiny sea snails.

There she meets six seahorses,

Clinging to reeds to beat the waves' forces.

Seven slippery fish swim all around her,
Zipping this way and that. Not one of them flounders.

Far out in the ocean, she passes a whale

With eight barnacles holding tightly onto his tail.

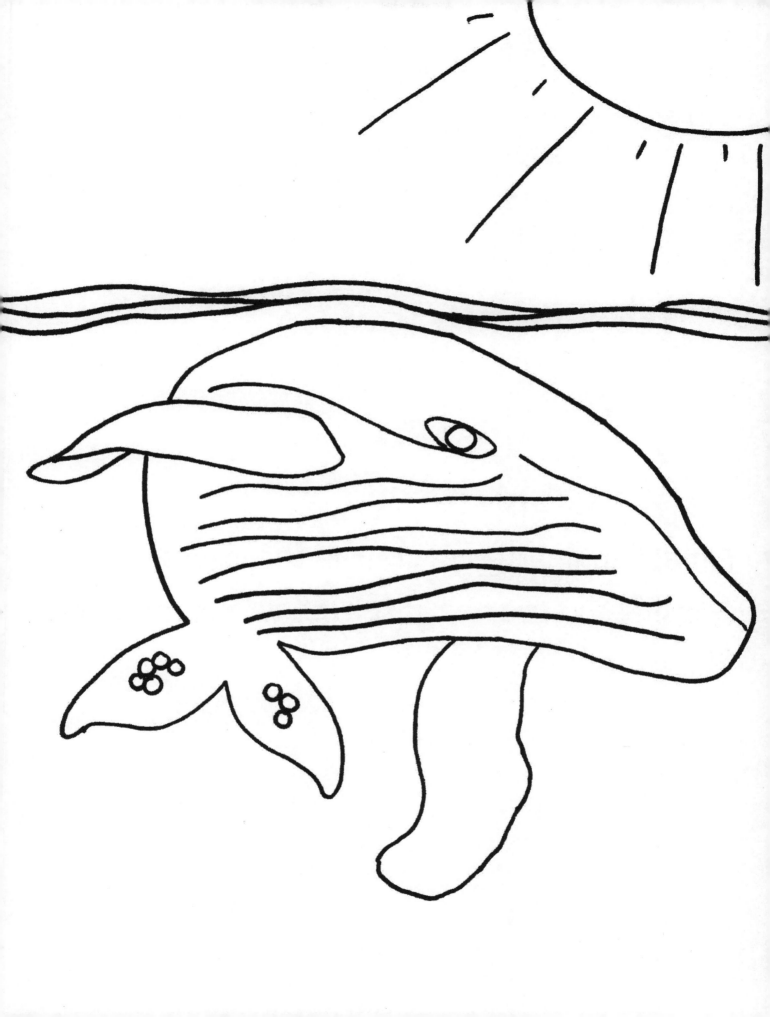

Nine dolphins play tag out in the waves.

Giggling and clicking as they show her the way...

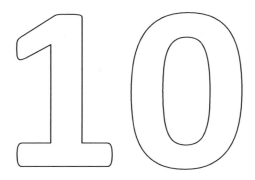

To where ten turtles are waving to her from afar,

Asking her to come join them right where they are.

With her friends and her family, she's here at last,

Swimming through currents and having a blast.

Christina Van Starkenburg is an award-winning writer. Since she spends a lot of her time reading and colouring with her two young boys, she decided to make a book where they could enjoy both activities at once.

Christina lives in Victoria, British Columbia with her two sons, her husband and their cat Philip. Visit her at www.thebookandbaby.com for more fun activities.

90007617R00020

Made in the USA
San Bernardino, CA
04 October 2018